The Purringest Kitty Finds His Home

Story by Rita M. Reali

Illustrations by Dee Lynk

Contact the author via email: **Rita@LittleElmPress.com**. Or visit **www.RitaMReali.com** for news about upcoming events.

For Tab, without whom this book would never have been possible.
And for Frank, who loves that silly cat more than he'll ever admit.
– R.M.R.

Special thanks to my husband Scott, my daughters Courtney and
Moriah, my son-in-law Leo and my two grandsons for your patience and
encouragement while I was lost in this project – I love you guys!
Thank you, Rita, for writing this adorable story and allowing me
to illustrate it. You inspire me with your creativity and perseverance
as you tackle one dream after another. You are one of a kind,
dear friend – the cannoli in a sea of yellow cake!
– D.L.

Rita M. Reali
The Purringest Kitty Finds His Home
Paperback: 978-1-7368236-0-6
Ebook: 978-1-7368236-1-3
First American Edition: February 2023

The Purringest Kitty Finds His Home

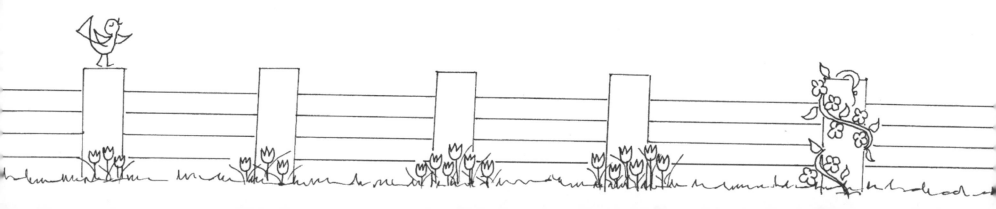

One warm summer morning,
a stripey butterscotch cat
appeared in the front yard
of a pretty yellow house.

The cat said,
"Moww."

The lady replied,
"Moww."

The two "Moww"ed back and forth at each other for a few minutes.

Little by little, the cat inched closer to the lady, until she was able to reach down a hand for him to sniff. But she didn't try to grab him or even pet him. She wanted him to know he could trust her.

The cat sniffed at her hand. He rubbed against her hand. He started purring.

prrrrrrrrrrrrrrrr

Then he let the lady pick him up.
He settled right into her arms
and purred even louder.

"Are you my cat?"
the lady asked.

The cat rubbed against her chin.

"Moww," he replied, which meant, "I am my own cat, thank you very much, nice lady. But I would be happy to live here with you."

Then the lady asked
the magic question:
"Are you hungry?"

The cat replied,
quite predictably,
"Moww."

The lady knew that meant "yes." She set the kitty down in the grass and went back into the house to find something for her new friend to eat.

She returned with a sad-looking, unopened bag of cat food she'd purchased in hopes a cat would come to visit her pretty yellow house.

She opened the bag and put a handful of dry kibble into a little pile on the stoop.

The cat didn't mind that the food was old. He was hungry. He gobbled it down.

When he finished, the lady poured out a little more food.

The lady's husband brought a bowl of water, in case the kitty was thirsty.

He was. "Moww," he told the man politely.

The man and the lady realized that meant, "Thank you."

The cat began to lap up the water.

Soon, the lady had to go into town to run errands. She kissed her husband goodbye and gave the kitty a pat on the head, then walked to her little blue car.

The cat followed.
"Moww?" he asked.

"No, I'm sorry," the lady said,
sounding sad. "You can't
come with me."

The cat jumped into the
little blue car anyway.

He climbed into
the lady's lap,
where he purred
and purred.

"Sorry, Kitty," the lady said, and lifted him out of the car.

When she started the car, the engine sound frightened the cat, and he skittered away.

As she headed down the driveway, the lady felt certain the cat would wander off after he finished his water... and that made her feel bad. She dearly wanted to keep him, but she figured he was probably someone else's pet.

Some hours later, the lady came home from running her errands.

She headed toward the house with her parcels and, out of a wishing kind of hope, called out, "Kitty... oh, kitty cat."

The cat, who had
been napping on
the wide front porch,
heard her call and
ran to greet her.
His long furry tail
waved, tall and proud,
behind him.

The lady dropped her parcels and scooped up the cat to hug him.

PRRRRRRRRRRRRRRRRRRRR

He settled into her arms, purring and purring.

But when the lady tried
to set him down again,
the cat put his paws
around her neck
and hung on.

The lady smiled. She knew, although the kitty had insisted otherwise, he *was* her cat. And *he* knew he had found his home.

CPSIA information can be obtained
at www.ICGtesting.com
Printed in the USA
LVHW072343210723

753146LV00002B/7